I0551521

Definitely Santa

A Collection of Family Christmas Stories

Christopher Robin Smith

Cover by Ron Pereira
ronpereira.net

ISBN: 979-8-9871183-1-3

DEDICATION

To
my lovely
partner in life,
who shares my
passion for Christmas
and whose patience, diligence
and love is evidenced on every page
of this book.

Thank you and Merry Christmas, April Biggs.

CONTENTS

INTRODUCTION

Many years ago, we began a family tradition: instead of sending out cards for the holidays, I wrote a story, and we sent that out to family and friends. The stories, a little fact and mostly fiction, were based on my Christmases past in Cleveland (where I grew up) and New York City (where I began my professional life).

For more than two decades, our family has had the honor of being part of another holiday tradition: Celebrity Centre International's annual Christmas Stories, a live charity show that raises money for the Hollywood Police Activities League's after-school programs and provides Christmas gifts for underprivileged children. Some of the stories in this volume were adapted from scenes and monologues written for those shows.

We wish you and yours a joyous holiday season and hope our stories become part of your family tradition.

Christopher Robin Smith

i

ONE FARE
CHRISTMAS
EVE

don't usually drive my taxi on Christmas Eve. But a couple of years ago, I decided to go out. My folks moved to Florida, and I can't take hot weather in December. My only brother, him and his family moved to Minnesota. Now, I can take the cold, but that's tundra temperatures out there. So, I was alone in the city. I figured driving would give me something to do, and besides that, I was a couple of hundred simoleons shy of the rent—three hundred seventy-seven and seventy-five cents, to be exact.

Let me tell you, Manhattan becomes one enormous Christmas decoration during the holidays. Everywhere you turn—store windows, lamp posts, bus stops—they all have a bow, string of lights, or something that says it's Christmas. Looking up Fifth Avenue, even the traffic lights, turning from red to green, look like they were planned as part of the holiday decor.

So this one Christmas Eve, I made my way up Fifth Avenue, figuring I'd get some high-brow fare at one of the high-brow hotels. You know, if you can afford to stay at the Plaza or the Sherry-Netherland, you can afford to drop a substantial tip on your cabby. At midnight, the streets were practically deserted. A few hours earlier, it was bumper to bumper, horns honking, the sidewalks packed with last-minute shoppers. But now, nearly no one at the corner of 34th Street and 5th Avenue—a hundred stories up the top of the Empire State Building was lit red and green. At 42nd Street and 5th Avenue, the lions in front of the public library, wearing those huge wreaths around their manes, were silent. And as I made my way uptown, I found the tree at Rockefeller Center as alone as I was.

By the time I passed the Plaza, the chances of getting a passenger looked pretty slim. Then I saw him right near the entrance of the Central Park Zoo—a guy in a Santa Claus suit hailing a cab. Well, it takes all kinds, and the one thing New York City's got is all kinds. This guy was waving like crazy. I was gonna pass him by, but hey, it was Christmas Eve.

Before I could even stop, he's got the cab door open. He yells to me, "Open the trunk. I'm in a hurry." At first, I thought to myself, "Who does this guy think he is?" Then I realize, who knows, this might be a trip to the airport—that'd be good for a few bucks. I jump out and open the trunk. This guy's got bags of stuff like I've never seen before. I've got a big trunk, but I wound up having to tie it closed. And we put a bunch of stuff into the back seat and more up in front with me.

By the way, this guy was wearing the best Santa Claus

2

outfit I've ever seen. Beautiful. I mean the fur collar, the belt, the boots, the whole deal. And if that beard wasn't real, I'm not a Yankee fan. I know a guy, another cab driver, who dresses up like Santa every year. A bunch of us pitch in, buy a case of canned hams, and he goes to the shelters and places like that and gives them away. I always thought his outfit was good, but this guy had him beat hands down.

We get into the cab, and he tells me to start driving. We get about a block, he yells for me to stop. So I stop. He says he'll be right back, grabs a couple of things from the trunk and disappears into this building.

Once he's gone, I notice how quiet it is. I mean silent. When you live in New York, quiet is a scary thing. When nothing happens in New York, that usually means something's about to happen. I figured I better step out and keep an eye on all the stuff in the trunk. Well, just as my foot hit the pavement, I hear the passenger door slam. It's him. He's back. "Let's go," he says. I pop the car in gear, and we don't go half a block before he yells to stop again. He's out before I can even stop all the way. I jump out of the car. I mean, that kind of thing is unsafe, right? He's rummaging through the trunk. "Hey," I says to him, "are we gonna be making a lot of stops?" "Yes," he says. "Well, I'd appreciate it if you wait to get out until I stop," I tell him. I'm not embarrassed to say I was a bit steamed. He says, "I'm sorry. I'm just in an extreme hurry," and disappears into another building. Hey, what do I care? The meter's running.

Well, before I know it, he's back in the cab. The routine keeps on going—we stop at the next building, and then the next, and the next, and the next, and the next. Every time he's in the trunk, into the building, and back lickety-split.

After a few blocks, I figure I've got it down. I step on the gas and stop at the next building. "Keep going," he says. I'm thinking, "What is with this guy?" I look up and notice the sign—Temple Beth-Israel. "Hanukah's over," he says, "keep going."

A few stops later, I'm looking at him in the rearview mirror, and I noticed, for the first time, a little trickle of blood on his forehead. "Hey buddy," I says to him, "you all right?" He nods. "Had a little accident," he says. "There was a new building on the skyline," he says. "Wasn't on our maps," he says. "We wound up right near the zoo. That's when you picked me up," he says. "Anybody hurt?" I ask. "Just a little shook up," he says.

We keep moving up and down the island of Manhattan. Then we hit Queens, Brooklyn, the Bronx, and even Staten Island. Covered a lot of ground. And I drove him into some pretty rough neighborhoods, too. I was a little nervous, but he says, "Don't worry about it." So I didn't. Everything turned out all right.

The sun was just coming up when we got back to the zoo. The trunk was empty. Nothing left in the back seat, nothing left in the front seat. When I turned off the meter, the fare was eight hundred seventy-two dollars and twenty-five cents. He hands me a wad of bills and says, "This should take care of it." He heads back into the park, and I yell to him, "Hey, who are you anyway?" He turns, looks at me, and then laughs.

After he disappeared into the park, I look down and count the money—twelve one-hundred-dollar bills. The guy gave me a three hundred twenty-seven dollar and seventy-five cent tip!

Every Christmas Eve since then, I take my cab out. I hang out on Fifth Avenue near the park, just in case. And you know what? I don't care what anybody says... I believe. I believe I might just get Santa Claus in my cab again.

CHRISTMAS
COOKIE
WEEKEND

ana is what I called my grandmother. Family legend has it that's what I said when I was a baby because I couldn't pronounce "Grandma." I never believed that, though. I distinctly remember calling her "Grandma" from the start. Maybe my mother and father just heard me wrong.

Our family baked cookies every year. It was a production called "Christmas Cookie Weekend," and "Nana" was the producer, director, and star. We waited all year for "Christmas Cookie Weekend." It began on Friday night and ran straight through until Sunday dinner.

My older brother and I were Nana's crew. She barked the orders, and we followed them diligently. I remember being amazed that she knew every recipe by heart. She never wrote them down, but she never missed an ingredient. "Three cups of sugar," she'd yell, and my brother and I would start measuring. "Four cups sifted flour," and we would sift away.

"Separate six eggs" always led to disaster—yolk, white and eggshells in two bowls instead of one, but she let us try just the same.

When we were finished, there were about two dozen "dozens of cookies"—less those that had been "accidentally" broken along the way. We had no choice but to eat those. "Taste testers," Nana called them. As for cookie variety, there were candy canes made of braided red and white dough, thumbprint cookies rolled in walnuts and topped with apricot jam, and "snowballs," bite-sized balls covered in powdered sugar. The last batches were always your basic cookie wreaths and trees sprinkled with red and green sugar. When the last cookie sheet was washed and dried, we helped Nana make an "assortment tray" for the dessert at Sunday's dinner. We'd wrap the rest of the cookies in wax paper and pack them into the cookie tins that once contained store-bought cookies and "Texas Manor Fruit Cakes." We put the cookie tins into the freezer, where they sat in suspended sweetness until Christmas Eve.

The final project on "Christmas Cookie Weekend" was decorating the tree. In our family, Nana's tree was always the first to go up and the last to come down. We would carefully remove each cherished ornament from the partitioned box, unwrap it, and, with grand ceremony, place it on the tree. The very last ornament was always reserved for me. It was a turn-of-the-century red glass St. Nicholas that had been given to Nana by her grandmother on her first Christmas. St. Nick still was finished with perfectly white paint to suggest the fur cuffs of his suit, the tassel on the end of his cap, and his beard, of course.

The hanging of this treasured ornament was a

tremendous responsibility, one which had been handed down to me by my mother. First, the heirloom was taken from its box, and the yellowed tissue paper peeled away layer by layer. Then the wire hook was carefully re-attached. Before putting it on the tree, I would take St. Nick over to Nana, as I did every year, and hold him up to her. She would gently kiss the old man on his rosy nose, and then I did the same. Then I hung the ornament in its place of honor right in the center of the tree. With the cookies baked and the tree decorated, our job was done. Nana sent her weary soldiers home to return on Christmas Eve.

"Christmas Cookie Weekend" didn't happen this year. After a long and mostly happy life, Nana left us last January. She didn't say goodbye; she just closed her eyes and went to sleep on a snowy evening in the New Year. She missed seeing my little Valentine, Sarah, born the next month.

I'm sorry that Nana's not around for Sarah's first Christmas. My little one will never have the chance to measure sugar, sift flour, and try to separate eggs for Nana.

The other morning, I entered the living room and found Sarah crawling toward the Christmas tree. She didn't notice me. I stood in the doorway as she looked up at the tree in all her innocence and wonder. I couldn't tell for sure, but from where I was standing, it looked like she was staring at Old St. Nick. After a minute or so, Sarah rose on her knees and reached for the fragile ornament. I was about to call out to her not to touch it but stopped. With a grace I'd never seen from her, she softly lifted the ornament from the tree. I stood and watched as she took St. Nick to her lips, gently kissing him on the nose. She then delicately placed him back on the tree. Her job done, she lay down and slept contentedly on the tree skirt beneath the tree.

Maybe those cookie recipes aren't gone after all.

Nana Smith's Thumbprint Cookies

$1/2$ cup butter
$1/4$ cup brown sugar
1 egg yolk
$1/2$ teaspoon vanilla
Cream these ingredients together and then add:
1 cup flour
$1/4$ teaspoon salt
Roll into 1-inch balls. Dip in slightly beaten egg white and then into finely chopped pecans.

Place an inch apart on a cookie sheet. Bake at 375 for 5 minutes.

Remove from oven and make thumbprints in the center. Return to oven and bake for 8 more minutes.

Fill thumbprint with apricot pie filling.

Recipe also works well doubled!

MY DAD HAS TO WORK

ver since I can remember, the holidays have been a dreaded though inevitable ritual. I watched with a sinking feeling in the pit of my stomach as the floats at Macy's Thanksgiving Day Parade kicked off the holiday season. I saw the vast display of holiday lights and finery tacked to every available surface, from the suburbs to the heart of downtown. Blinking lights and animated holiday figures left me cold, not just because of the temperature outside.

In school and later at work, my colleagues would ask me about my holiday plans. Doing anything special for the holidays? Would I be spending time at home? Is the family getting together this year? Will you be opening your gifts on Christmas eve (as some anxious revelers do) or waiting until Christmas morning? The answer was always the same... "My dad has to work."

I feel guilty that I resented it so much. I mean, I know business goes on even during holiday time. Year after year after year, he worked straight through the holidays. There were some years that I practically didn't see him for the whole month of December. My mother tried to console me, but ultimately his absence took its toll on her too. Here was my father, revered as one of the most giving men around, leaving his family alone on Christmas. As the head of an enormous manufacturing and distribution company, I guess there's little time for idleness. He could have taken some time off, but it was a tradition with him. He just couldn't see it any other way.

When I went away to college, I just stayed away. I wasn't out of touch. I just didn't make the long trip home for the holidays. It was easier that way. I didn't have to go through the disappointment, and Mom didn't have to watch the scenario play out as it had for so many years.

I have a family now. Last year was our first Christmas. On Christmas morning, my wife, my son and I sat beside a warm fire opening the gifts beneath the tree. My son was only nine months old, but I felt he appreciated that I was there with him. My wife did, and I know I certainly did, too. I have to admit, though, even then, I kept picturing my dad slaving away.

Well, over the last year, I've been doing a lot of thinking. Dad's not getting any younger and won't even think about retiring. Anyway, I've decided that this year I'm going to miss out on the holidays at my own home and spend the time with my dad. Since my dad has to work, I'll go to work with him.

You're the first to know. I haven't even told Mom yet. So, on Christmas, while you're tucked in your beds, I'll be sitting on your rooftop in the sleigh while Dad makes his way down your chimney. And for the first time in my life, I'll hear my father say, in person, "Merry Christmas to all, and to all a good night." I think somehow my son will understand.

LIVING IN LONDON

This story may have been overheard in a restaurant in Beverly Hills or Manhattan. It may have been...

nnie Grieves? I never told you about her? I can't believe that. I met her in London when Tom and I went there a couple of years ago. I never told you?

Well, every day while Tom was working, I'd see the sights. You know, the usual—the National Portrait Gallery, the Victoria-Albert Museum. But I didn't just look at the art, I looked at the people. You know, I figure you really get to know a place when you get to know the people. So, I'd wander through the galleries watching, wondering who they were, where they lived, what kind of jobs they had...

It was Christmastime, and I went to Harrods, one of my

favorite people-watching places. I guess you could call Harrods a department store, but it's more than that. It's an institution, really. Been around a couple of hundred years. The Queen buys her towels or soap there, that kind of thing. It's not just the Macy's crowd, if you know what I mean.

Harrods is this great huge building covered with lights. Every corner, every edge, and every windowsill is lined with white lights. It might be like that all year round. I don't know. But they looked like Christmas lights to me. And Harrods has this Food Hall where they sell... food. But it's not like a grocery store. They've got delicacies and caviar and wine and cheese.

That's where I first saw her. She had on this three-quarter-length mink. Beautiful coat. Beautiful woman. She was probably 70 years old and had a Harrods shopping bag on one arm and her purse on the other. Huge purse. You know, a massive purse. And she looked familiar somehow, like I knew her from someplace.

She was staring at the fish sculpture. Well, it's not really a sculpture. It's more like a design made of fish. They have this colossal case with ice, and then the fish are all arranged in a design, all the different shapes and colors and sizes. And it'll look like a starburst or something. Different designs. It's beautiful. You can't believe it's just dead fish. It's so beautiful.

So, she was standing there staring at the dead fish sculpture, and it looked like she was crying, not like bawling crying, just like getting-misty crying. Well, that's hitting the jackpot when you're people-watching because then you get to wonder what she's thinking of, what's making her weepy. I looked her over carefully, and I saw that part of the lining of her coat was hanging out from the bottom like the hem was worn. And she put her hand up to her cheek, and I saw the hem on the sleeve was the same way.

She must have stood there for five minutes which may not seem like much, but that's a long time when you're just looking at a design made of dead fish.

She finally stepped away and started shopping. I followed her around the store and kept watching. She'd take things off the shelf and put them in her Harrods bag—sardines, Stilton cheese, a bottle of port, a bottle of sherry, crackers. I'm thinking maybe she's having a party, maybe getting appetizers, you know. Then she gets to the chocolate, and she opens her purse and fills it… with chocolate. And, like I said, it was a massive purse. All the time, I'm thinking, I know this woman from somewhere.

When she finished, she headed straight for the exit. She didn't pay. She was just walking out! I'm watching this and I can't believe it. And before I know it, she's gone. I followed her, but by the time I got out on the street, she'd disappeared.

I told Tom about it at dinner, and he went on a jag about how the cost of theft gets passed down to the consumer, so "ultimately, we're paying for the old bird's shopping spree." He missed the whole point. I know this woman from somewhere. That's what I get for marrying an economist. You tell him anything, and he finds a way to turn it into some financial analysis.

Now, you know, one of the rules about people-watching is that if you want to see someone again, you go back to the place you saw them, at the same time of day. People have routines, I guess. So, I did. I went back to Harrods the following afternoon.

She was there. Same mink. Same bags. Same misty-eyes. She must have been at the tail end of her dead fish design stare because she started shopping right after I got there. She's filling her bags with stuff, and all the time, I'm wracking my brain to figure out how I know her. And I'm trying to imagine who's eating all that chocolate. She could not do it alone.

She gets loaded up and right out the door like that's how it's supposed to be. I ran after her and watched her cross the street. I couldn't get across in time, so I lost her again.

Well, this went on for four days. And I'm like an addict—rushing to Harrods to get my shoplifter fix. Then, one day, she's just about to go out the door, and some security guy stops her. He was plainclothes, but he flashed some Harrods badge at her. He takes her aside, and I make my way over to them, pretending to look at these jars of olives so I can listen to what they're saying.

I hear the guy say, "Ms. Grieves," and that's when it hits me. It's Annie Grieves. You remember her from the secret agent books? She wrote I don't know how many. I used to read them, all of them, and I recognized her from the picture on the back of her books. Anyway, I'm thinking, oh, my god, it's Annie Grieves.

She says to the security guy that she just forgot to pay, that it was so busy, she got distracted. She rattled off excuses like crazy. He says he understands, she can go ahead and pay, and they'll forget about the whole thing. Well, she can't open her purse because it's filled with chocolate, so she's fumbling through the pockets of her mink like she's looking for money. And I know she doesn't have any. She's just stalling.

It was so sad. I loved this woman's books. And I hadn't heard anything about her for years.

So, I take a hundred-pound note out of my purse—Harrods isn't cheap—and I crumple it in my hand. I step a little closer, bend down, and I come up with the bill and say to her, "Excuse me. I think you may have dropped this." She looks at me, and without even blinking, she says thanks and hands the bill to the security guard. The two of them head for the cash register, and that's that. End of story.

I went to Harrods the next day. No, Annie Grieves. I saw the store detective guy. He was there, but she never showed up. And I waited for an hour. It was weird. I missed her a little, as if we'd somehow become friends.

A couple of years later, we were back in London at Christmastime. Tom was doing some conference, so I headed to Harrods. I went back to the Food Hall to see if maybe, somehow, I might see her again. I waited and looked around, but she wasn't there. I stopped and stared at the dead fish sculpture for a while. It is fantastic.

Anyway, I left the Food Hall and went into the main store, and there's a long line of people waiting for something. I look ahead and see this poster, a book signing. Yeah, Annie Grieves. Isn't that something? So, I got in line. When I got closer, I could see her—a little older but just as beautiful. And at one point, while I was waiting, she looked up, and I swear, she looked right at me.

When it was my turn, I stepped up to the table. She looked at me and said, "We've met, haven't we?" I just nodded. What was I going to say? She took a book, and she signed it for me.

I waited to get back to the hotel before I opened it and

read what she had written. "Sometimes you don't even know you're lost until someone finds you. Thank you. Merry Christmas," signed Annie Grieves.

And inside, like a bookmark, stuck in the pages, there was a hundred-pound note. I left it in the book, right where she put it.

DOROTHY

don't even remember the first time I watched her work. I must have been around seven or eight. But once I saw her, I was hooked. She was the lady who wrapped presents at The May Company, and to me, she was a genius.

This was no throw-some-wrapping-paper-over-a-box-and-stick-a-bow-on-it sort of operation. This woman elevated the wrapping of presents into an art form.

She had sample wrapping jobs hanging on a pegboard wall behind her. Each color scheme was without fault, and a suitable decoration accompanied each ribbon and bow. I remember the rattle for the baby shower gifts, a plastic pipe for Father's Day, an array of miniature reindeer, wreaths, and Santa's adorned her sample packages at Christmastime.

She wore a smock—the uniform of a professional gift wrapper. It was aqua, and while no one looks good in aqua, she managed to pull it off. On her lapel was pinned a nametag. "Dorothy," it read, and below her name, the number of years she had worked at The May Company. The first time I recall reading the number, it said "17."

Dorothy reverently took your purchase from you and asked you to choose a style from the pegboard. If you paused for even a moment, she was quick to come to your rescue. She might ask questions about the person for whom the gift was intended. Then she would make a suggestion, always the right one and always in exquisitely good taste.

Her first job was to snip off the price tag discreetly. She checked two or three times to ensure that the cost of the garment or whatever it was would remain a mystery to the recipient. She then eyed the size of the gift and chose the box most perfect for the job. Now, I'm sure she only had a few box dimensions to choose from, but the care with which she went about this business led me to believe that she had a storeroom brimming with boxes, increasing in size by mere millimeters.

Her next task was to line the box with tissue, something she did most earnestly. The paper exactly lined the box, perfectly covered the gift, and had just the right amount of overlap on top. She then affixed a gold sticker embossed with The May Company logo to fasten the loose edge of the tissue paper. I never took out a rule to measure, but I'm sure if I had done so, I would have found the gold sticker positioned precisely in the center of the box.

Then she made her way to the large spools of wrapping paper, pulling out just the right length. The sound of the paper slicing along the cutting edge sent chills down my spine as a child—it was so precise.

She went on to cover the box with paper. She pulled it so tightly that I was sure it would tear at the corners. But it never did. The folds she made on the ends were crisp and exact. And the flap, which was eventually neatly taped in place, was as intricate as an origami swan.

Dorothy took special care with the ribbon. She crossed the package, making the horizontal and vertical cross at an exact intersection, sometimes in the upper left-hand corner, other times square in the middle.

And Dorothy made her own bows, each one a masterpiece. Like a magician, she took the stiff ribbon, looped it around her fingers, and with a wave of her hand— a perfectly shaped bow appeared. I wasn't the only one who gasped out loud when she finished her trick.

As Dorothy's services didn't come free, we only had her wrap a select few Christmas packages. Every year, each family member got one "Dorothy Special." And no matter how many gifts were stacked under the tree, Dorothy's presents always stood out.

After I grew up and moved away, every trip back home for the holidays included visiting The May Company and Dorothy. The last year I saw her, her nametag read "Dorothy" and below: "Thirty-seven Year Employee." Her hands were stiff and bent with age, but her bows never revealed her pain—each loop as perfect as ever. The hours passed like minutes as I watched the magnificent Dorothy wrap box after box.

Her job responsibilities at The May Company had been expanded to include manning the "Returns Counter." I saw a sense of disbelief in Dorothy's eyes as she took the exchanges, as though the act of returning a gift was a betrayal. To a person to whom the presentation of a gift was sacred, returning one was, I suppose, an unthinkable deed.

I didn't know then that would be the last time I saw Dorothy. The following year I found a "Self-Serve Gift Box Center" where the gift wrap had been for so many years. None of the other store employees had much to say other than Dorothy had gone home sick one day that winter and had never come back.

Through a curtain, I could see the storeroom behind Dorothy's old workstation. Behind the clutter of empty crates, packing material, and stacks of self-serve boxes, I spied the corner of a pegboard. I made my way over to it, and there they were, like works of art haphazardly stored and forgotten in an attic—Dorothy's sample packages. I carefully pulled the two I could reach off the pegboard—one a candy cane with an elf hanging from the bow and the other a metallic red package beautifully contrasted with green holly leaves.

Every year I put those packages out amongst the other presents, a silent tribute to the lady who wrapped presents at The May Company. And no matter how many gifts are stacked under the tree, Dorothy's presents always stand out.

ALONE

 felt alone that Christmas. It was true, I was surrounded by my family, but still, I felt alone.

It had only been a few weeks earlier that my son had left home, headed to the city to start a new career. I felt the emptiness where he once stood.

"Some men came by today," he told me. "They want to give me a job—a job in the city. And I'm going to take it."

I went numb at first. I had heard those words before. About fifteen years earlier, when my son was just a child, his father had come to me and said the same thing. I didn't say a word then. I wished I had, but I knew it probably wouldn't have changed his mind. He said he would come back for us once he was settled in. My husband left for the city and never came back.

I don't think I could have gone with him to the city. My roots are here, in the country.

I stood limp as my son's words echoed through the generations. I didn't say a word. I knew it probably wouldn't change his mind either. He was his father's son. And like any good son, he looked up to his father and wanted to grow up to be just like him.

Well, he is grown up, I told myself. He's old enough to make his own decisions. It is his life.

Still, his leaving stung like the bitterly cold winter winds.

On that Christmas morning, I heard the children laughing loudly as they played in the snow that fell the night before. I heard the sounds of their happiness and watched their delight in a world of white. It reminded me of my son. No one enjoyed the snow more than he did. He hated the heat of the summer months, the dryness. The snow made him come to life. While others around him withered at the sight of the first snow, he embraced it. He loved to be covered with it. I wondered if I would ever look at snow without thinking of him. The children laughed on, long and hard.

A year passed by, from spring to summer to fall to winter. With another Christmas approaching, I thought of my son. The snow began to fall, and I thought of him. I heard the laughter of the children, and I thought of him.

One afternoon I heard men's voices in the distance. It reminded me of the voices of the men I'd heard, the ones who had come and taken my son off to the city. I strained to listen to what they were saying, hoping to hear my son's voice amongst the crowd. But as they got closer, I realized my son was not with them.

"Hello," I called out to them. "Over here. You came by last year and talked to my son. He went with you to the city."

The men nodded and said they remembered the boy.

"Take me to him. I want to go. I want to go to the city."

They smiled, not in a mean way, but in a way that told me they wouldn't take me to him.

"There's no place for you in the city," one of the men told me.

"But my son. I want to join him there."

Another man shook his head. "It wouldn't be right for you. Your son fit right in, perfectly."

"But I feel so alone," I said.

"Alone?" said one of the men. "How could you be alone? You're surrounded here by your family."

I looked around, and he was right. My family was all around me.

The men turned and began to walk away. One of the men came back and said to me, "You'd be proud of him."

"Would I?" I asked.

"He is the best that ever went to the city from around here."

"He is?" I asked, wanting desperately to hear more about my son.

"He is. He's the most perfect Christmas tree the city's ever seen. You know, they planted him right in the city square. Right next to the other tree, the older one."

His father, I thought to myself.

The man smiled as he spoke. "Out here, they were beautiful. But back in the city, all on their own, no other trees around, they're majestic. Filled with lights and decorations, their branches covered with snow. Perfect."

The man tipped his hat to me and joined the rest of the group as they continued walking out of the woods, back towards the city, leaving me behind.

A moment later, the snow began to fall lightly, and I thought of my son and my husband. I heard the children's laughter and thought of them. But I didn't feel alone anymore.

LET IT SNOW

hat do you mean it doesn't snow there? That's how I responded when I was told we were moving to California. As an eight-year-old boy expecting to live a full and rich life on the tundra known as Cleveland, this news came as a devastating blow.

My mind raced through the myriad of white-covered activities I had experienced in my young life. I thought of the toboggan on the golf course and my near-fatal crash into the sand trap; as it was, I only lost a tooth. I felt the cold squeak against my jacket as my sister and I made angels in the fresh canvas of our backyard. I tasted the clean snow in my mouth, the frozen shrapnel of a snowball I caught while laughing. I saw my tiny dog, Taffy, burrowing through a drift, only to emerge baffled by the mound of snow on his snout. I even longed for the back-breaking sensation of shoveling the stuff off the driveway. I was old enough to know that life wasn't fair, but this tragedy illustrated how thoroughly the odds were against me.

No talk of the ocean and beaches or the proximity to Disneyland could pull me out of my depression. It all came so suddenly. My mother told me I could make new friends. I knew that. Friends are a dime a dozen, whereas a perfect act of nature is a dear commodity and one that would be impossible to replace.

We had three more days until Christmas and five more days before the contents of our home on Priscilla Avenue were packed into a truck, and we boarded the plane for the West Coast. My father may have been getting a promotion, but he never even considered that he was depriving me of a vital element of childhood. It was easy for him to leave it all behind. He had already lost the magic of snow. When I looked out on a snowstorm, I saw a vast and beautiful adventure. When he looked out, he saw only traffic jams and slippery roads. When I saw snow, I thought of the exhilaration of a day spent in the white-capped suburbs. When my father saw it, he thought of the cold and flu season.

Well, I made the most of those last five days. I am sure I approached beating Admiral Byrd's record for consecutive hours spent on a frozen landscape. I had no dog sled, but I had Taffy, and he loved the snow as much as I did. Fueled by the warmth and sugar of the hot chocolate my mother doled out every few hours, I was sure I could survive in this climate indefinitely.

I spent most of my last day burying various pieces of trash in the snow. It was sweet revenge to think about the yard as the snow melted in the spring, covered with rusty soup cans, empty soda bottles, and soggy Christmas wrapping and ribbons.

As we drove to the airport, I rolled down the window to suck every last breath of winter before leaving Cleveland forever. That lasted only a short time before my father "persuaded" me to roll it up. I held my cheek against the window instead as I munched on the Christmas cookies Mom had packed for the ride.

The year flew by in California. As my father predicted, I did love it. We had a great yard with a pool to swim in all year round. However, I was reminded of my dear friend winter as December approached. It got cold for a few days and it did rain, but rain was not snow and a skateboard was not a sled.

I started watching the weather report on the news each evening in hopes that the weatherman would share some footage of a great Midwestern blizzard. I saw snow a few times on the news, but it was always from my father's viewpoint, with traffic jams and slippery roads. No shots of the magic.

On Christmas Eve, it got to me. All the snowy Currier & Ives wrapping paper, the snowman candles on the dining room table, and the miniature plastic house that lit up and played "Let It Snow" were grim reminders of my frozen friend.

I went into the backyard, fixed my gaze skyward, and yelled at no one in particular, "It just isn't Christmas without snow." I looked around, grateful that my family hadn't heard me.

Suddenly I felt something on my cheek. It was barely perceptible, but something had definitely landed on my cheek. I touched my face and as I pulled away, on the tip of my index finger sat a snowflake. A single snowflake. A snowflake that could have been the model for a Christmas tree ornament. A perfect snowflake.

Its majesty and beauty overwhelmed me. The shock had caused me to hold my breath. I exhaled with a whoosh, and the warmth of my breath melted that solitary flake in an instant, leaving behind a tear.

I looked into the still blue sky, flicked the moisture into the air and ran back into the house.

OVERSEAS

The following are the contents of two letters written on the same day in 1922, at precisely the same time, one in New York and one in London.

My dearest Samantha,

Oh, how I wish I could be with you right now. I feel such a fool to have missed the ship.

I got out of my taxi and ran the last half mile, with my luggage banging against my body, but alas, I was still too late. If you had seen my face as the ship pulled out from the dock, you would have no question about the sorrow and disappointment I am suffering now.

My only Robert,

Oh, how I wish you could be with me right now. You are such a fool to have missed the ship. If you could see my face as I write, you would have no question about the sorrow and disappointment I am suffering now.

Your telegram was quite short and to the point. "SAM. MISSED BOAT. MISSED CHRISTMAS. LOVE, ROBERT."

In addition to the overall disappointment regarding your message, I took exception to the fact that you addressed me so informally. You have never called me "SAM." If I didn't know you better, I would have thought that you abbreviated my name to save a few shillings, but I am sure it was your attempt to create some endearment meant to soften the blow of your succinct cable.

I am sorry to have addressed you so informally in my telegram greeting. I had less than two pounds in cash in my purse. In anticipation of my return to the states, I spent nearly all of my English money so I wouldn't have to bother converting it back to dollars. At any rate, the balance of your name added fifteen pence to the tally. I knew I would follow my telegram with a long letter and that everything would be forgiven.

My darling, I keep imagining you curled up before the fire in the drawing room, your eyes sparkling with the reflection of the flames, your soft white skin, as pure as freshly fallen snow, cuddled up to my shoulder.

Ah, the smell of your sweet hair. Oh, how I wish I was with you right now.

It has been quite a day. I started a fire in the drawing room. Apparently, a squirrel's nest had fallen down the chimney and clogged it. Well, before I realized anything was amiss, the room was filled with smoke. I tried to open the damper, but my efforts were rewarded only with soot. I was covered from head to toe. Even after a long bath, I smell like smoked ham.

Father is very upset with you. He says that any man who misses his boat is not fit to work for his newspaper.

To cool his temper (and save your reputation should you ever get around to proposing marriage to me), I offered him an acceptable explanation. I assured him that while I know you did not intend to miss the sailing, that this sort of experience was precisely the fodder a great writer needed, that you would manage to turn this misfortune into a humorous and poignant essay for The Ledger. I told him, knowing you, that your first letter to me would probably serve as a rough draft for such a piece of non-fiction. He agreed and is as anxious as I am to receive the postman each day.

I'm afraid to leave the house as I am sure he would open your letter without me. He so loves your writing.

I am sure this mishap is just the kind of thing that your meddlesome, blowhard father has been waiting for to dash my newspaper job _and_ my engagement to you in one fell swoop. Forgive me for being so blunt, but if he weren't your father, I wouldn't like him one bit. I am willing to go toe to toe with him over your hand, and as far as his newspaper job goes, The Star is by far the more prestigious of dailies in town anyway. I shall take a position with them.

As the next ship for New York doesn't leave until the twenty-sixth, I have accepted an invitation from my dear friend, Robert Earnsley. His fiancé is French, as you may recall. When he heard of my plight, he insisted that I accompany him so I wouldn't have to sit alone in some lonely hotel on Christmas Eve.

If I find any solace at all, it is in knowing that you will be sitting alone in some lonely hotel room on Christmas Eve. My family is going to my brother Jack's house for Christmas.

Mother and Father were quite insistent that I come along, but I told them I couldn't dream of having a good time while you were off in some foreign land alone. I can't bear the thought of celebrating while you sit and suffer.

Robert's fiancé has a younger sister, and I have been told that I will have to be her escort for the entire holiday. From what I hear, I will be paying a dear price. She is just eighteen and is such a bother to her parents that they will not allow her to have anyone call on her.

According to Jack, if they allow one man to see her, they will be mobbed by young men, as they were last summer on the Riviera. I will suffer in silence and do my host's bidding.

I now regret having taken my trip so close to holiday time. In the future, I shall declare a moratorium on any travel during the entire month of December. In fact, to be on the safe side, it will be our agreement not to travel from Thanksgiving Day straight through the first of the year. I vow never to be away from you during the holidays as long as we both shall live.

Oh, Robert, how could you have taken a trip so close to the holidays?

In the future, I forbid you to leave the county from Thanksgiving Day straight through the first of the year.

I vow that you will never be away from me during the holidays as long as we both shall live.

I so look forward to New Year's Eve. I am sure you will be back by then. I dare say if you aren't, you can just forget about any engagement. I will never speak to you again if you are not with me in time to greet the New Year.

As I mentioned, the next ship out of England is on the twenty-sixth. Unfortunately, that will bring me back to New York on the third. I am more sorry about missing New Year's Eve than I am about missing Christmas. I was hoping to ask a certain girl to marry me that night. We will have to plan our own New Year's Eve sometime at the beginning of the month. I'm sure you will forgive me.

I honestly don't know if I could forgive you for missing New Year's. I will hate you forever.

I will love you forever if you forgive me.

You not being home for Christmas is unbearable, but even more so as it heightens the suspense of what gift you will be giving me. And I will be absolutely furious if you buy me kerchiefs as you did last year. I am sure it will be some exotic item one can only buy in England. I hope that it is something from Harrods.

Since we're missing Christmas anyway, I might as well tell you what I bought you, so the suspense isn't unbearable. I went to Harrods to buy you something special. Well, they had the most beautiful kerchiefs, far more excellent than those I bought for you last year. The irony of the purchase was that when I returned to my room, I noticed a small imprint on the box- "Imported from the U.S.A." And to think, I went to England to buy them! Isn't that funny?

I shall pose a riddle about the gift I bought for you. It is something that has ticks but is not a dog.

It is something that is wound but is not yarn. It is something that you will pass the hours with but is not your beloved.

I am rather excited as my parents are giving me a watch. This old one I have is responsible for my missing the boat in the first place.

It is something that will see to it that you never miss another boat. I'm sure you've guessed by now.

I am posting this letter today. At this late date, and with the holidays in full swing, I can only hope it reaches you before I do.

I adore you.

I am mad for you.

Don't let us ever be separated on the holidays again.

I will see you on...

...New Year's Eve.

...the third of January.

Until then, I am yours...

Love, Robert.

Love, Samantha

SUBSTITUTE
SANTA

This story is dedicated to Isaac Hayes, for whom it was written and who performed the story of Mr. Haines before an enthralled audience.

t was 1951, and I can assure you, no one was more shocked than I was when they asked me to put on that Santa outfit. Mrs. Watson came running into my office half crazy. Seems Old Bill Davenport, who was playing Old Saint Nick, had come down with the old flu. No matter how much chicken soup those elves pumped into him, it looked like Old Bill was out for the season. He'd been Kramer's Department Store's Santa for as long as I could remember. He sort of "grew" into the part. He started off having to wear a pillow under his costume, and a few years ago, the gal in the sewing department had to let out the seams.

Anyway, Mrs. Watson went on and on about how Bill

couldn't play Santa and they had no replacement. I asked her, "How about Mr. Goman in ties?" "He's only one hundred and ten pounds. He'd have to sit on the children's laps!" she said. "Mr. Holland in shoes," I suggested. "Too bashful," she said. Every name I mentioned, Mrs. Watson, had an ironclad reason they could not play Santa Claus.

Suddenly, like she'd been woken up from a deep sleep, she looks at me. I asked if she was all right. She just stared. I asked if she wanted a glass of water. She just stared at me. Then she started looking me up and down, up and down. Just as I realized she was eyeballing my suit size, she blurted it out. "Mr. Haines, will you play Santa Claus?"

Now, I know a lot of things, and somewhere at the top of the list was that I was not the man to play Kramer's Department Store's Santa. Mr. Kramer loved Christmas. It wasn't just the business—and the store was crazy busy at Christmas—he believed in the tradition and stuck to it like ice on a windshield. Well, a traditional Christmas season at Kramer's did not include a black man wearing a long white beard and a red suit.

I apologized to Mrs. Watson and begged off her offer, but she was insistent. I told her that I wasn't quite sure that the customers at Kramer's were ready to break with tradition. "Mr. Haines," she implored, "if there is no Santa, black or white, sitting over in that big chair in ten minutes, there won't be any customers at Kramer's. They'll all load up their families and drive over to McCullough's. And, well, you know, Kramer's and McCullough's are the Macy's and Gimble's of South Jersey."

Mrs. Watson and I went back and forth for a long time, and somehow, at the end of it all, I was dressed as

Santa, sitting in that big chair at exactly nine a.m. as Kramer's opened its doors.

The first little boy came up and sat on my lap. "What's your name?" I asked him. "Robert Sherman," he replied. "And what do you want for Christmas, Robert Sherman," I asked. Although I'd never been Santa before, I had been a kid. I figured the only way to be a good Santa was to listen to the children. "I want my own wagon. I have to share my brother's wagon, and I hate him." "Well, Santa only brings gifts to good little boys and girls," I said. "Well, I guess I don't hate him. I just want my own wagon." I told him Santa would see what he could do about it and gave his mother, who was within earshot, a wink. Each child that came up got the same treatment. I listened to each one as if he were the only child I'd seen that day. I remember that's how I felt when I sat on Santa's lap. No other kid in line mattered.

The morning went on without incident. I sat there waiting to hear the shouts of some angry parent or the wails of a disappointed child. It never happened. As the hours went by, my "Ho, ho, ho's" got a little more confident until they echoed through every department of Kramer's. Mrs. Watson stood close by. The biting of her lip was replaced with a smile and, once in a while, a tear.

Then, at about eleven thirty, Mr. Kramer's head poked up through the crowd. Now, I'd seen him mad, like the time the night watchman left the gardening shed open and some kids had covered the place in peat moss and sand, but I'd never seen him mad like this. He was trembling. He waved at Mrs. Watson, and they disappeared into the office. I thought I heard screams, but I couldn't be sure. There's a lot of noise in a department store.

I waited for them to come and remove me from my commission. They never came. I had a lunch break. They never came. When I got back to Santa's chair, the line just seemed to get longer and longer. If I had one child sit on my lap, I had a hundred. But no matter how long the line, I listened to each one like he was the only one. There was little David, Joel, Krystina, Hadley, Emily, Jenny, and Gregory. Each one had their own wish for Christmas, and from the smiles and nods I got from the parents, didn't look like those kids would be disappointed on Christmas morning.

Late in the afternoon, I had just finished listening to a little boy named Noah. I saw that he was there with his nanny. The nanny's son, a little black boy, was hiding behind her. "Ho, ho, ho," I bellowed, "come over here little boy and tell me what you want for Christmas." Well, it was hard, but we finally peeled him off his mother and got him on my lap. I asked him his name and what he wanted, and he told me his name was Irving Hopper Jr. and that he would be happy with whatever his mamma could get him. I asked him, "What would you like from Santa?" He was silent. I asked him again. Nothing. "If you could have anything you wanted, what would you want?" He finally said, "I want a baseball glove. Just like Jackie Robinson's." I looked over and his mom gave me a faint smile. I told Irving Santa would see what he could do.

I finished up the day at around seven o'clock. My knee was a little sore, but I was smiling. As I headed back to my office, I realized that I'd have to stay late to get the inventory done that I had missed that day. There was Mr. Goman and Mrs. Watson and Mr. Holland and Mr. Kramer taking inventory. Mr. Kramer stepped out front. "Mr. Haines," he said to me, "you may have saved Kramer's this Christmas." He went on to say that when he saw me in the Santa outfit he was ready to fire me, Mrs. Watson, and anyone else who knew about it. He said Mrs. Watson had convinced him to watch me work, which he did for the better part of an hour. "Santa is Santa," he said, "no one noticed." They all agreed. "No, no one noticed," I said. He told me that sales were up, and as far as he was concerned, I was officially the new Santa Claus at Kramer's Department Store.

Now, I have a little confession to make. I told Mr. Kramer a little lie that day. At least one child had noticed that Santa was... different. As I lifted one little boy off my lap, he leaned over, touched my cheek, and whispered, "I always knew." Before I left that day, I went upstairs to Kramer's sporting goods and picked up a baseball glove, just like Jackie Robinson's. And ever since then, I've been Santa Claus at Kramer's Department Store.

WRONG
NUMBER

Academy Award nominee Anne Archer brought her elegance, grace and sublime talent to a story written especially for her, a story about how it's never too late to make up for missed chances.

t was Christmas Eve last year. I'd been to two parties that day – nothing special just friends and whatever. Then I stopped off at my sister's. She was wrapping presents, baking and the usual. I stayed until about two and still had to get up at the crack of dawn to get over to my brother's house for Christmas morning.

I was exhausted. The kind of I-don't-even-remember-my-head-hitting-the-pillow exhausted.

And then the phone rings—4:30 in the morning. My mind is racing a mile a minute. At first, I'm not sure if it's the phone, my alarm, or a school bell. You know, it's the middle of the night.

I zero in on the phone and start to think of all the bad things this call could be: dad's in the hospital again, or there's been an accident. You don't know. With all that was racing around my mind, it seemed like ten minutes, but the phone only rang a couple of times.

I picked it up and there's a man's voice on the other line, and he says, "Is this Nancy Upton?"

"Who's this?" I said.

"This is Brian. Brian Reiner."

"Do I know you?" I asked.

"I think we went to high school together," he says.

I told him I didn't think I went to school with a Brian Reiner and asked him how he got my number.

He said that he was thinking about Nancy and since he knew he was in the phone book, he figured she was probably in the phone book, so he called the first Nancy Upton in the book.

"Well, you got the wrong number," I told him.

Then it dawned on me that it was 4:30 in the morning on Christmas day, and why would anyone ever call anyone at that time of night? So, I asked him.

He let out a deep sigh and told me. He said that his Nancy sat in front of him in World History. Every day while Mrs. Burgson rattled on about Visigoths and Vandals and Huns, he was looking at the back of Nancy's head. He said he loved her hair, the way it laid across her shoulders and how every hair fell into place to form a neat arrow pointing down her back.

And he said that once in a while, while she was thinking, she would turn her head a little, and he would see her cheek, and even though he'd never touched her, he imagined her skin was softer than anything he'd ever felt.

Well, this wasn't quite what I was expecting. At first, I was going to hang up. I mean, it was just weird. Not "weird" weird but "odd" weird. The shock of the phone ringing had woken me up and I figured I was probably up for good, so why not talk to the guy?

I went into the kitchen to make a pot of coffee and asked him if he was so in love with Nancy, why didn't he ever tell her?

He said he tried to a hundred times, but he couldn't. Sometimes when they'd both get to the end of the aisle going to their seats, he'd step aside and let her go first. But then he'd have to wait for her to put her books down and sit at her desk before he could pass and sit down. And in that time, all the things he could say to her would race through his mind, but nothing ever came out. He'd just nod and pass by and take his seat behind her.

He said she was so smart. She'd always ace their tests, and he'd even tried to cheat off of her a couple of times when he wasn't sure of the answer, but he didn't.

"And her handwriting was impeccable," he said.

"Okay," I said to him, "so you were in love with her. What are you calling her tonight for?"

Another deep sigh, and then he said that he'd had a rough year. He got into some trouble at work and he almost lost his job, but it all worked out—had to do with some accounting error and somebody tried to pin it on him. He wound up standing up for himself, and if he'd just kept silent, which is how he'd usually handled things like this, he would have lost his job for sure.

When he did that, it got him thinking of all the times in his life when he didn't speak up, of all the opportunities he might have missed because he was too whatever to say something.

And when he thought about all the times he'd wished he'd have said something, he kept coming back to Nancy Upton. He thought even after all these years, he just wanted to tell her how he felt. He finally just wanted to talk to her.

We were on the phone for, I don't know, maybe another hour. He did most of the talking, and that was all right. He told me more about his Nancy and all these other times he'd almost spoken to her.

There was this whole thing with the prom that went on for weeks. He said it was kind of corny, but he was going to ask her, but he figured someone had already asked her. He found out later that no one had, or at least she didn't say yes to anyone, so she wound up not going to prom either.

In the end, talking to Brian Reiner wasn't weird or sad. It was just a guy finally getting something off his chest. And I was glad that he'd dialed my number and that I'd picked up the phone at 4:30 in the morning.

By the time we hung up, it was almost 6:00. He thanked me for listening and apologized for calling. I told him it was no problem, that I'd had half a pot of coffee and was pretty wired anyway. Then he hung up.

I don't know why I didn't tell him who I was. The more he told me, the more I wished I had—the more I wished I'd spoken to him back in World History and that I knew he liked me, but I didn't know what to say back then. And how I'd sometimes pretend to be thinking and turn my head a little when I was really just trying to get him to notice me.

I don't know why I didn't tell him that night that I'd lived a life of unspoken dreams, always too afraid to speak up and always regretting that I didn't.

I sat for a few minutes and finished my last cup of coffee. And then I went and got out the phone book, and there he was, Brian Reiner.

I called him later that same Christmas day. I told him that what he'd said had touched me and that I would never miss an opportunity again.

I told him that I was his Nancy Upton.

I FORGOT
CHRISTMAS

 FORGOT CHRISTMAS!

I can't believe it. I forgot about it. I've been working so furiously for the past three weeks I didn't even notice Christmas was coming.

Oh, every day I saw that massive sign on my way to work that said, "TWELVE DAYS LEFT, ELEVEN DAYS LEFT, TEN DAYS LEFT...." I thought they were talking about how much time I had to finish the Philips account. I am such an idiot. The people in my office must think I'm nuts. Last week, I came in and demanded to know who hung that sign and that it seemed an awful extravagant way to keep me on schedule. They just stared at me. For a long time. I finally just walked back into my office.

Well, it's not like the Christmas decorations gave it away. I mean, they've been out practically since Halloween. The music in the elevator, those clanging bells, the white snowflakes hung over every intersection with the wreaths and candy canes on the light poles. Those things do not mean "get ready for Christmas." They are not there to let a person know that the biggest holiday of the year is approaching. They are there as a constant reminder that you have to shop.

I DIDN'T SHOP!

I haven't bought a thing for anybody. Not a thing!

Okay, I'll just make a list and get it done. It's December twenty-third. That leaves me several... hours. How could I have done this?

Well, I guess I can throw that stack of catalogs away. Even with express delivery, it's too late for that now. Oh, and I had folded down a page with a gift for my brother John. It would have been a great and memorable gift. I was going to buy him one of those radios where you can listen to any station worldwide. I mean, you can get England, Greece, Germany, you name it. I know he'd love it because he doesn't get to travel as much as he did when he was single.

His wife! His kids! I have to shop for them, too.

Jenny, Jason, James, and Jackie. Oh, I wish he hadn't done that thing with the names so they'd all have the same initials. I guess I could buy the whole family a set of monogrammed towels, wrap them separately, and give one to each.

This is so contrary to how I was raised. In our family, you took weeks to shop. And you only bought a person something that was exactly right for them.

One year my brother and I overheard our mother complaining about her tea kettle: "It's old. It doesn't even whistle anymore. It just sort of sputters." Well, that was all we needed to hear. We set out that Christmas to buy her the tea kettle to end all tea kettles.

Every time we went to the store, we headed straight for the kitchenware section. We studied the selection of kettles for weeks. And when we got home, we talked for hours, arguing about the benefits of one over the other. We finally decided on the perfect tea kettle. It was white enamel with a pattern that, we felt, matched Mom's kitchen decor exactly. And it came with a lifetime guarantee. Sure it was expensive, but we had a Christmas Club account, meaning money was no object.

Man, I haven't thought about Christmas Club accounts for years. Not for years.

That year, as we got closer to the holiday, we made our huge withdrawal—about sixteen dollars—and bought that tea kettle.

When we got home, we wrapped it immediately. Then, after a few days, John came to me and said he thought we had used the wrong wrapping paper and that the candy cane striped paper was "more motherly" than the elf paper. So, we unwrapped the kettle and wrapped it in the new candy cane paper. We did that three more times with three different kinds of paper. My mother never could figure out how we went through so much wrapping paper that year.

On Christmas morning, we were dying for Mom to open the box. We didn't even care about our gifts as much as we wanted to watch her get that new tea kettle. She carefully removed our fifth wrapping job, opening the gift with grand ceremony, and, holding the treasure in her hands, she said the magic words—"It's just what I wanted."

She got six tea kettles that year. I guess a lot of people

heard her complaining. However, she returned all of them except ours. She still has it.

Oh, I've got so much work to do. And not on the Philips account. On the Christmas Club account, thank you very much. Whatever they sell in catalogs, they must sell in stores. I'll finish my list on the way downtown. Only one day left. I can do it.

I really did forget Christmas.

WHAT ARE YOU GONNA DO?

hristmas Day in Manhattan, late afternoon. The diner was empty except for one waitress, one cook and one customer. The customer sat at the counter, nursing a cup of black coffee.

"Can I warm that up for you?" asked the waitress. The customer shook his head.

"You look beat," she said to him. "Long day, huh? It's been quiet here." She swiped a wet rag across the counter. "I'm glad you came in, gives me somebody to talk to. Dimitri, he's the owner and the cook back there, he doesn't speak much English. Nice fella' though. What are you gonna do."

She went on talking to the stranger as she lined the catsup bottles in a row on the counter, carefully balancing them, one on top of the other. She told him how she'd bet Dimitri that business would be slow, that people would stay home on Christmas. "I don't think he knew what I was sayin', so we're open. Lucky for you, I guess. Sure you don't want anything to eat? Today's specials are gonna be tomorrow's soup and there's gonna be plenty of it." The customer shook his head again.

"I told the other girls I'd cover today. They've all got kids and families." She told the stranger that her son was a grown man and lived out in California. Her husband was down in Florida where he'd taken a job a couple of years earlier. "I don't know how he does it. I went down but I couldn't take that heat. I didn't stop sweatin' until I got back to Queens," she told the man at the counter.

"He's not coming back up here and I'm not going down there. And they say California's even hotter. What are you gonna do."

"I guess I'm not goin' anywhere. What would my regular customers do without me? I got lots of 'em who I think come in here just for me. I can't take all the credit. Dimitri's a pretty good cook, and you can't beat the prices. But some of 'em come in here just for me."

She spoke about one man who had come to the diner nearly every day for the past nine years for breakfast and lunch. He always sat in the same booth and if it wasn't open, he'd wait. "I try to reserve it for him, but once in a while somebody sneaks in when I'm not lookin'." The man's name is George, and he ordered the same thing—poached egg, dry wheat toast in the morning, and tuna melt in the afternoon. "Can you believe that?" she asked the customer. "He's not odd, just particular." George worked somewhere near the diner and lived up in Westchester. "He's a real nice man. We always talk. You know, I work here and everything, but I think he'd say we were friends. Let me get you a little more coffee," she said, reaching for the pot.

"George lost his wife last year," she said as she poured. "He didn't really talk too much about it. Got a couple of kids—a boy and a girl. Anyway, he's a regular. I got a lot of regulars."

She looked down at her watch and, noticing the time, picked up her pace. The customer started to get up from his stool. "Stay right where you are," she told him. "I've got lots to do before we close. And there's a whole pot of coffee I'm just gonna pour down the drain if you don't drink it."

She yelled into the kitchen at Dimitri to turn off the neon sign in the front window. "The sign. Off the sign," she said as she motioned to him. "You'd think after all these years he'd learn the language. Funny. Good cook, though. What are you gonna do."

She told the man at the counter that George, the regular customer she'd been telling him about, had invited her up to Westchester for Christmas dinner that night. She guessed she could probably get on the train and still make it there on time. "I was thinkin' about takin' one of those chocolate layer cakes," she said, nodding her head toward the dessert case. "I decorated it up with holly leaves. That's all icing. I think the kids would like that. Anyway, I don't know if I'm gonna go." She collected all the cream pitchers from the counter. "More cream?" she asked her customer. He shook his head. "No? You're all set? Okay."

She told him the trip to Grand Central and the train ride to Westchester didn't excite her, but the thought of spending Christmas with a couple of kids did. "You know, it's really for the kids, all the decorations and gifts and everything."

She pointed out the garland, ornaments, and lights she had strung all over the restaurant. "The kids come in here, and their eyes just light up. You should see 'em. Some of the regulars get a kick out of it, too. It brings the kid out in 'em." She told him Dimitri liked her decorations because they spruced the place up a bit.

"I guess I should go see George," she said as she unscrewed the tops off the salt and pepper shakers. "He's a real nice guy, you know. I'll take the cake, and I've got a couple of things for the kids, too." She said she hadn't bought them anything too big, just a little something. She had a girlfriend who worked at Macy's and she got her employee discount. "Hey, every little bit helps," she said, shrugging her shoulders. "Anyway, thanks for listening. To tell you the truth, that's all I wanted for Christmas. Just somebody to talk to. What are you gonna do."

She turned back to the kitchen and yelled again for Dimitri to turn out the light. She motioned to him again, pantomiming turning the switch and frantically pointing toward the neon sign. The light finally went out, and with the humming of the neon sign silenced, the diner got very quiet.

The stranger sat for a moment, watching her as she filled the salt and pepper shakers and screwed the tops back on tight. He pushed himself up from the counter.

"Well, you have a good night," she said to him. "Hey, by the way, that's a beautiful Santa suit you got on. That's one of the good ones. Very authentic. Merry Christmas."

The bell on the door rang as the stranger left the diner. She yelled back to Dimitri to let him know it was only the two of them left and that she would lock the door. She acted out locking the door, but Dimitri didn't understand. She threw up her arms and went and locked the door.

As she cleared the counter, she noticed that the customer hadn't left any money for his coffee. "Well, it's Christmas," she mumbled to herself.

When she lifted the cup, she found a small piece of paper. She picked it up and inspected it. "It's a train ticket... to Westchester... with my name on it." She thought about it for a moment, and then, as she slipped the ticket into the front of her apron, she said to herself,

"What are you gonna do."

DEFINITELY SANTA

y family moved to Cleveland, Ohio, when I was three. Before that, I lived in Toledo. For a three-year-old, there was little that changed in my life after the "big move." All of my toys were packed into the truck, and I held on to "Sandy," my doll, for the ride in my family's silver car.

I had a beautiful room in the new house. But it was pretty much the same as my room in the old house. My door was a few feet farther from my parent's bedroom, my bed was a few feet farther from the door, and the hallway and steps downstairs were covered in a thick, soft carpet. Other than that, things felt the same as always.

That all changed at Christmas time that year. My family piled into our new car, a deep green car with soft fabric seats. As we headed downtown, the slush slapped the side of the car. Public Square exploded with an overwhelming array of lights. The Soldiers and Sailors Monument was lit up red, and the wrought iron fence around the monument was decorated with wreathes swaddled in red ribbons. An enormous snowflake of white lights hung over the street just beyond. I remember I didn't speak. I felt like crying, but I didn't. I strained to open my eyes as wide as possible to take in as much of the spectacle as possible.

A few minutes later, I was carted from the car into the cold and then into the heat of Sterling-Linder, a department store on one side of Public Square. Once inside, I stood before a sight that outdid the outside decoration by a hundredfold—the tallest Christmas tree my family and I had ever seen. "Nothing like that in Toledo," my father said, "It's seven stories tall." The tree rose from the ground floor up through the store's atrium. The Sterling-Linder interior magnified the tree's majesty. I could see people looking at the tree from the balconies stacked on one side of the store.

By the time we got off the elevator onto a floor near the top of the tree, my mother had taken off my winter coat. A cool breeze touched my cheeks as I bravely looked down. The tree was twice the size from up there.

I had been brought here to see Santa Claus' village. It was my first visit to the old man. My hair got a good combing, and the bow on the front of my dress was re-tied. My father picked me up, gave me the same kind of kiss he gave me when he left for work each morning and sat me gently on Santa's lap. The red suit was soft and lined with even softer white fur. My eyes started at the beard and moved upward to the smile, the rosy cheeks, and finally, the old man's eyes. I just stared at his blue eyes. They were gentle and kind. In them, I saw the lighted monument, the snowflake, the tree.

In his eyes, I saw Christmas.

Santa asked me what I wanted for Christmas. I tried to speak, but no words came out. All I could do was think very hard about the things I wanted. Santa said that since I was a good girl, he would surely bring me everything I wished for. His eyes glistened as he spoke. He gently lifted me from his lap, and I stepped down the platform into my mother's arms.

As we left, I looked down at the tree once more. On the way home, I sat silently in the car as my family "ooohed" and "aahed" over the snowflake and the monument. I thought only of the sweetness of the old man's eyes.

That Christmas, Santa delivered everything I had wanted. All the images that had passed through my mind while I sat on his lap magically materialized under the tree in my house. This was the work of Santa. Definitely Santa. I tried to tell my family about the old man and my wishes and the gifts under the tree, but all that came out was, "Merry Christmas."

Our family made the trip downtown the next year and every year after that. And every year, we marveled at the sights in the square, which grew a little more sophisticated each Christmas.

Every year the Sterling-Linder tree got more impressive. And every year, Santa Claus' eyes got gentler. There was no question in my mind that this Santa was the same man, year after year. His eyes were as much a part of my memory as anything.

I never spoke. I only thought about what I wanted, and he always assured me he would bring me everything I wished for. Every year my dreams appeared beneath the Christmas tree.

The year I turned sixteen, I made the trip downtown on

my own for the first time. When I set out that day, I didn't know whether I would see Santa or not. After all, I was practically an adult. I shopped all day, but in the back of my mind I thought only of Santa.

It was late in the day when I decided to go to Sterling-Linder. The store was closing, not just for the night but forever. There was no tree, no crowds looking down from the balconies—just a confusion of the remaining "Going Out of Business" merchandise.

I rushed to the elevator. The doors opened to what had always been Santa's village. But it was just a floor covered with racks of picked-over clothes. On the shelves along the far wall were a few remaining ornaments from the colossal tree.

As I stepped out of the elevator, I looked to the end of the balcony and saw him. Standing, waiting, an old man with a soft white beard. He wore no red suit lined with fur. No hat. No shiny black boots. His eyes brightened as I walked toward him. He cleared his throat a few times but never spoke. His blue eyes welled up with tears. We stood in silence. I hugged the old man and held him.

I took a long look into his blue eyes and thought of every Christmas since that first one, every Christmas morning and the miracles under the tree.

I turned and walked to the elevator. As the doors opened, I looked back. He stood there, still. "Thank you," I said as the doors started closing, "Merry Christmas."

ATTABOY,
CLARENCE!

Nancy Cartwright, best known as the voice of Bart Simpson, delivered the following make-believe confession before a live audience. Attaboy, Nancy!

I have a confession to make. Until last week, I had never seen the movie, It's a Wonderful Life. I know it's shocking, but it's true.

For years I avoided it. I had lots of reasons why I had never seen it, reasons which I explained to many dismayed people I met along the way. Some of the stories were standard like we weren't allowed to see movies as kids because my parents didn't want us to eat candy, or I had an eye condition and dark theaters increased my chances of blindness. These only worked on strangers because I'm constantly sucking on a piece of hard candy and I go to movies all the time.

I had a few more creative excuses that I developed over the years. One had to do with my mother. I used to tell people that my mother had been a childhood friend of Donna Reed, who played Mary Bailey in the film, and that when Donna left for Hollywood, she left without even saying goodbye to my Mom. I explained that my mother was so hurt by this that, out of loyalty, we couldn't bring ourselves to watch her old friend on the big screen. Some people believed me. After using that one for years, I started believing it myself. I used to have dreams at holiday time about Donna Reed coming over to our house, arms filled with big gift-wrapped Christmas presents, and patching things up with my Mom.

My best story was that I couldn't see It's a Wonderful Life because my father was in military intelligence. I told people that my father had worked in a covert operation along with Glenn Miller, the Big Band leader. My father posed as a coronet player in Glenn's band. I told them that my Dad's actual function was communicating messages to undercover guys in the audience through a sort of modified semaphore signal, for which he used his horn instead of flags. After I had them going, I said that my father narrowly missed getting on the plane that fateful day when Glenn went down over the English Channel. Now, Jimmy Stewart had the misfortune of playing both George Bailey in It's a Wonderful Life and Glenn Miller in The Glenn Miller Story. Shut them right up.

The real reason I never saw it was… I didn't want to be disappointed. People have been recommending movies, books, plays, you name it, to me for years, and nine times out of ten, I wound up disagreeing with their glowing reviews. I used to think maybe I was too critical. Then I thought maybe it was because most of my friends had terrible taste. Of course, I realized that thinking that my friends had terrible taste was the same as being too critical. Anyway, I had heard so much hype year after year about It's a Wonderful Life that I didn't want to be the one who saw it and didn't like it. That distinction would somehow make me less... human.

Last week I went to a movie with a girlfriend at one of those places that show classics. We were supposed to be seeing a Garbo film. Seated dead center in a packed-out theater, surrounded by people and giant tubs of popcorn, the lights dimmed and the movie began. Then the title, It's a Wonderful Life, lit up the screen. I don't know how I missed it. I was trapped. There was no way to get out of my seat. I began sweating like you do right before you take a big test or go into an important interview. My girlfriend saw the terror in my eyes. She had heard the Glenn Miller story many times. I thought to myself, "Did she do this on purpose? Did she trick me into watching It's a Wonderful Life?" It didn't much matter. I was about to watch the Christmas classic I'd avoided for years.

I was still sitting in my seat sobbing when the ushers opened the doors for the next show. My friend sat silently beside me, afraid to speak. As the new audience started filling in around us, I was frozen. I didn't exactly choose to watch it again, but I did. Maybe I was making up for lost time.

My eyes were still bloodshot the next day, but I was filled with a sense of self-satisfaction. My friends didn't all have terrible taste, I wasn't so critical after all, and... I was definitely human.

Since that day, I haven't gotten to the end of a banister without checking to see that the thing-a-ma-jig at the end was attached, just like Jimmy Stewart does in the movie.

I get misty when I hear Auld Lang Syne.

I once went to a Beverly Hills High School swim meet to see the famous "jitterbug pool."

I even got a subscription to National Geographic.

And every time I hear a bell ring, I know an angel gets his wings, and I say to myself, "Attaboy, Clarence."

ALONE IN A CROWD

he thought of spending another New Year's Eve alone was unbearable.

Ernest was invited to a couple of parties; one at the home of a friend from work and one at his cousin's. He turned down both invitations.

He'd tried celebrating with friends from work in the past with disastrous results. It was all so cliche, with a few too many having a few too many and embarrassing themselves. The experience made him feel as if he'd been trapped inside a New Yorker cartoon come to life.

The cousin scenario was an even more dismal prospect. Two years before, Ernest welcomed the New Year at his cousin's apartment. The party ended abruptly when the police came, and his cousin was arrested for disorderly conduct, the culmination of a little disagreement he had with his brother. After the police hauled the two of them away,

Ernest was stuck getting rid of the revelers and the empties, both of which seemed to cover every square inch of the apartment. Since then, his cousin, a stockbroker by trade, had done quite well for himself, which only meant the party, the excess, and the argument with his brother would be excessively more excessive.

The couple across the hall invited him over, "Nothing special. Just a few friends." Getting to know your neighbors that well seemed to go against the most basic rules of living in Manhattan. He imagined being cajoled into playing charades with them and wanting the throttle the wife for continuing to guess "Gone with the Wind!" even though the category was "Song Title." It was easier to tell them he had other plans.

For weeks he chewed on the problem, trying to decide where he would be when the clock struck twelve. And then, on Christmas Eve, it came to him. It was too obvious. He would go to Times Square.

Sure there would be thousands of people there, but unlike at his cousin's house, he was sure he wouldn't have to clean up after any of them. Sure it'd be cold, but no colder than his empty apartment. Sure he'd still be alone, but he convinced himself that alone in a crowd is not really alone. It was settled—he'd spend New Year's Eve in the heart of the New Year's capital of the world.

Ernest planned it all out; he'd treat himself to lunch at Orso on Restaurant Row, then make his way over to Times Square in the late afternoon and secure a great spot to watch the ball drop. Reservations at Orso were hard to come by, and he figured New Year's Eve might be impossible, but he called anyway. The Maître d' was out, so the hat check girl picked up the phone. When Ernest asked, a sweet voice answered, "Getting a table for lunch is no problem. Dinner, now that's another story."

It was done—reservation for one for lunch on December 31st. He thanked the hat check girl and asked if she'd be working that afternoon. She said she would, and Ernest told her he'd see her then.

Ernest chose to keep his plans secret. If anyone asked, he just said he already had plans. He was afraid that if he shared his plans, someone would try to talk him out of it or ask him to tag along or look at him with that look people give other people when they're trying to cover the fact that they feel so sorry for them and their pathetically lonely life.

He imagined himself standing in the middle of Times Square, surrounded by hundreds of strangers. When the ball dropped, he would turn to the woman closest to him and kiss her, and she would turn out to be the woman of his dreams.

Each day Ernest grew more and more anxious to carry out his plan. When the 31st finally rolled around, he was like a caged animal. He took a cab from his apartment on the Upper West Side and got off near Columbus Circle. With all the streets blocked off, he walked the final stretch, making his way down 8th Avenue to 46th Street. It was a clear day but bitterly cold. Though he was breaking a sweat now, he knew that as the hour approached midnight, he'd be happy he'd worn so many layers of clothes.

Ernest had fantasized about meeting the hat check girl who took his reservation, that she would immediately be smitten with him, and he with her. She would tell him that she got off work at 9 o'clock and would meet him near the

TKTS booth in Times Square or some other agreed-upon spot, and they would kiss at midnight.

When he got to Orso and checked his top three layers, instead of a winsome beauty, he found a well-worn middle-aged woman. Her name tag identified her as "Helen." He asked if she had been the one who'd taken his reservation. "Nope," she told him in a voice that sounded like metal shavings, "Sounds like Emily. Got the day off." Ernest and Emily. Visions of monogrammed towels danced in his head, his fantasy foiled by a simple scheduling glitch.

Lunch was as he expected—delicious. Better than delicious. Mouth-watering, scrumptious... No, it was better than that. He gave up trying to put it into words. And the service was impeccable. Would he could afford to have lunch here more than once a year.

It was 5:30 when he finished lunch. He collected his things from Helen, wishing her a Happy New Year and stuffing a five-dollar bill in her tip jar. "You too," she rattled back at him.

When Ernest made it out to Times Square, it was packed with people. He had hoped to set up camp at the base of the statue of George M. Cohan, but that spot was already taken. He settled in front of a pizza place a few blocks uptown on 7th Avenue. It was one of his favorite spots. Beneath the massive blinking sign for the pizza shop hid one of Manhattan's lost treasures—the facade of the I. Miller shoe store. Here, suspended a full story above the sidewalk, were statues of the great ladies of the silent screen in the costumes of their most notable characters. Ernest stood directly beneath Mary Pickford, outfitted as "Little Lord Fauntleroy." He doubted anyone else even knew she was there.

The hours passed slowly. Ernest kept his feet spread wide apart to secure a few more inches of Manhattan for himself. At about 9:30, he watched from the corner of his eye a woman edge her way next to him. "It's her," he thought to himself, "This is the girl I'll be kissing tonight." She was a petite beauty with porcelain skin. He tried not to look straight at her as he busily rehearsed opening lines to himself.

"Excuse me," she said after stepping on his toe. He turned to respond and noticed that she had a dog in a small pouch around her neck. It was a Boston Terrier, and it was staring right at him.

He thought, "What kind of person brings their dog to Times Square on New Year's Eve?" Horrified, he realized that he'd spoken those words aloud. His eyes opened wide as if to disintegrate his statement midair somehow before it reached her ears.

"The kind that doesn't want to hear from her neighbors about how he howled all night," she said.

She didn't seem offended. Maybe it was all right.

She extended her hand. They shook. It was all right.

"I'm Emily," she said.

"Emily? " he asked. "You're not the hat check girl at Orso, are you?"

She nodded, a bit suspicious.

"You took my reservation... I spoke to you on the phone."

"I take a lot of reservations," she said.

He had hoped that his reservation was somehow special. It wasn't.

He told her he'd been there earlier for lunch and how

well Helen had taken care of him.

"Helen's worked on Restaurant Row since 1950," she told him. "First as a hat check girl, then a cocktail waitress, a waitress, a bartender, an accountant, and she finally retired in 2000."

Emily said that Helen had lived with a retired cop for years. When he died a few years back, she couldn't afford their apartment on her own. So, she had to go back to work. Now she fills in whenever they need her.

It was beautiful listening to Emily because it gave Ernest an excuse to look right into her eyes. They were green.

She went on to tell him that yesterday had been her last day at Orso and that she was moving on. A job in one of the department stores; better hours, better benefits.

"My name is Ernest," he said.

"Ernest? Really? That's my dog's name."

Ernest thought, "Great. I have the same name as her dog." He checked himself quickly. No, he hadn't spoken out loud again.

"I love that name," she said. "That's a name to be proud of."

Ernest looked at her, then at the dog and then back at her. Both were smiling.

The evening was shaping up very well. He looked up and noticed the time: 11:57.

The last two-and-a-half hours had passed in a heartbeat. He and Emily had talked about everything; their mutual love of the Frick Gallery, how tranquil Central Park West was early on a Sunday morning, going out just to smell the smell outside H & H Bagels on upper Broadway. It seemed as if they'd known each other forever.

"Did you ever notice the little statues behind the sign on this building? Mary Pickford?" she asked.

It was 3 minutes before midnight and he was standing in Times Square next to the woman of his dreams.

Someone set off a firecracker nearby and Ernest, the dog, jumped right out of his little harness and onto the ground. A frantic Emily searched for him.

"I'll get him. You wait here," Ernest, the man, told her.

He ducked down and spotted the dog in a sea of legs. Ernest, the dog, was making his way toward 7th Avenue.

Ernest, the man, chased him half a block. That he had stayed on the pup's trail was nothing short of a miracle. Ernest got down on his hands and knees, parting the crowd roughly as he made his way toward the dog. The dog froze, and Ernest reached and caught him.

Both Ernests' hearts were beating like mad. Ernest got to his feet, holding the dog tightly in his arms. When he came up, he saw that he was half a block from where he'd left Emily. He started in that direction when the countdown began.

10-9-8... There must have been ten thousand people between him and the pizza shop.

7-6-5... He made little forward progress.

4-3-2... Ernest, the man, looked at Ernest, the dog.

1... The crowd burst into celebration. Horns honked, confetti streamed, noisemakers noised.

Ernest the dog, his eyes wider than usual, licked Ernest the man's face.

Emily strained to look over the crowd. She couldn't see either Ernest. She'd lost them both.

On the large screen projected in front of the entire crowd, she saw her dog licking the man she had met just a few hours before.

Ernest saw himself on the screen. As the dog continued to lick, he mouthed, "Happy New Year" to Emily.

It was another hour before the crowd dispersed enough for Ernest to make his way to the pizza shop.

Emily was gone.

She must have gone to Orso. He struggled across the boulevards to the restaurant. When he got there, it was packed. Helen hadn't seen her. No one had.

Ernest stepped out on the street, still holding the dog. What started as the perfect evening ended in a perfect disaster. He met his Cinderella and instead of a shoe, she left behind her dog. He didn't know where she lived. He couldn't remember which department store she said she would be working in. She was gone. He had lost her.

His mind raced. He would go to a 24-hour copy shop, make posters, and put them up all over town. He'd start on the upper West Side and make his way downtown.

Ernest looked at the wide-eyed pup and patted him on the head. As he did, he heard a sound, like a little bell. It was the dog's tags jingling against each other.

Ernest pulled off a glove with his teeth. Holding the cold metal tags between his fingers, he softly read Emily's phone number aloud.

ABOUT THE AUTHOR

Christopher Robin Smith is a writer, actor and acting teacher. At fifteen, he began his professional performing career as a member of the Cleveland-based nostalgia band, The Fabulous Brylcreams. After attending Kenyon College and the University of Exeter, he moved to New York City, where he joined the award-winning improvisational company Interplay. Christopher and fellow Interplay member Jim Meskimen made several appearances on Whose Line Is It Anyway? As a writer, he's created material for John Travolta, Ashton Kutcher, Juliette Lewis and Al Gore, to name a few. With Tamara Wilcox-Smith, Christopher co-founded the National Improvisational Theatre in New York and, along with Eric Matheny and Tamra Meskimen, in 2006, founded The Acting Center in Los Angeles.

For more about Christopher, go to smithinla.com.

Thank you for reading Definitely Santa. *As an independent author, I primarily rely on word-of-mouth for exposure. If you have the time and inclination, please consider leaving a short review on amazon.com, goodreads.com or any other site readers use to discover their next favorite book.*